SUPER HAPPY PARTY BEARS
CRUISING FOR A SNOOZING

CRUISING
FOR A
SNOOZING

MARCIE
COLLEEN

【Imprint】
MAKE YOUR MARK

NEW YORK

{Imprint}
MAKE YOUR MARK

A part of Macmillan Publishing Group, LLC
175 Fifth Avenue, New York, NY 10010

Library of Congress Control Number: 2017945055
ISBN 978-1-250-12416-6 (paperback) / ISBN 978-1-250-12417-3 (ebook)

Our books may be purchased in bulk for promotional, educational, or
business use. Please contact your local bookseller or the Macmillan
Corporate and Premium Sales Department at (800) 221-7945 ext. 5442
or by e-mail at MacmillanSpecialMarkets@macmillan.com.

Book design by Christine Kell
Imprint logo designed by Amanda Spielman
Illustrations by Steve James

First edition, 2018

1 3 5 7 9 10 8 6 4 2

mackids.com

If this book isn't yours, keep your thieving paws off it.
Obey or may your cookies crumble EVERY TIME!

TO ERIN.
THE ORIGINAL PARTY BEAR.

CHAPTER ONE

Welcome to the Grumpy Woods!

Now make like a dust bunny and hop on out of here. And while you're at it, take a few bags of trash to the dump.

That's right. It's springtime and the Grumpy Woods is a disaster.

You might remember
that several months ago the
townscritters had a rollicking
Hibernation Eve celebration with
the Super Happy Party Bears. Well,
it's all fun and games until someone
wakes up and faces the mess.

As the very first robin sang

his "winter's-over-CHEERio,"
the townscritters popped their
heads out from their homes to
find mountains of soggy wrapping
paper, fruitcake crumbs, and
smashed gift boxes. Empty honey
jars and unraveled ugly sweaters
dangled throughout the newly

budding tree branches. It was enough to make everyone extra cranky.

At first, Mayor Quill simply declared Mayoral Decree number 3,456: *Clean up the Woods*. But

while this new decree was hung
on the tallest tree in the center of
the Woods, it was ignored. No one
looked at it. The critters pretended
they didn't see. Bernice Bunny—
the Woods's resident bookworm—
kept her nose down in her book
as she walked past. Even Dawn
Fawn, who loved to clean, refused
to sweep. Therefore, the Woods
remained trashed.

Finally, Mayor Quill held a very official meeting at City Hall, which is that upturned log over there. Everyone—from Squirrelly Sam to Sheriff Sherry Snake—attended. Except for the Super Happy Party

Bears. They were not invited,
because when the townscritters
are extra super cranky, it's usually
due to the bears.

At this particular meeting, it was
decided that new measures were
needed to clean up the Woods.

There was a lot of "Why are you
looking at me?" and "I didn't do it!"

Mayor Quill banged his gavel.
"Spring is a time of beginnings.
Therefore, I decree we all turn over
a new leaf of tidiness."

"I am not turning over *anything*!"
said Sam. "It was the Super Happy

Party Bears' idea to throw the
party. The mess is their fault."

"That's true," murmured the
crowd.

"We should make them doOOOO
the cleanup!" added Opal Owl.

"As party punishment!" said
Bernice.

"Mayor Quill isn't suggesting that we *do* the cleaning," explained Humphrey Hedgehog, the assistant deputy to Mayor Quill. "Just that we use our superior brainpower to come up with *how* to clean the Woods. Then Mayor Quill will insist the bears do the cleaning."

Sherry Snake suggested using the trash to stop up the holes in the crumbling Grumpy Wall.

"If it sssstinkssss, no one will even think to crossss over the wall."

That idea was quickly thrown out.

Humphrey presented a prototype of his Tremendous Slurp-tastic Vacuum-izer. One flip of the switch, however, and Mayor Quill's podium, all of Sam, and several of Opal's feathers were swallowed up. Perhaps the Vacuum-izer was a little too powerful.

The townscritters thought and thought. Finally, Dawn Fawn cleared her throat and stepped forward, clutching her copy of *The Magic of Cleaning Up*, which was usually tucked into her apron pocket next to her can of cleaner. The townscritters scoffed whenever she pulled out this book. But no one could ignore the fact that they had a big mess, and Dawn Fawn was born to clean.

She handed the book to Mayor Quill without saying a word.

"If it doesn't bring you joy," read the mayor, flipping through the pages, "it must be thrown out."

A murmur rippled through the crowd. "Joy? What's joy?"

The Magic
of Cleaning Up

"That's not important," said
Mayor Quill. "Just throw *everything*
out."

"That makes sense," murmured
the crowd.

The townscritters marched to
Party Patch, the Headquarters of
Fun, to give the news to the Super

Happy Party Bears. "Throw out everything that doesn't bring you joy!" they told the bears.

But, as you might have guessed, the bears found joy in everything— even cupcake wrappers and crumpled paper plates. Therefore, nothing changed. It seemed that the townscritters would have to take matters into their own hands—with rubber gloves on, of course.

And so, each morning, everyone in the Grumpy Woods woke up at the crack of dawn, grabbed their feather dusters, and ordered up some breakfast—a tall stack of "spick-and-span-cakes" with a heaping dollop of ACHOOO!

That is, everyone except for the Super Happy Party Bears.

Follow the carefully placed sticks, laid out in the shape

of arrows, up the flower-lined
path until you see a welcome
sign. That's Party Patch, the
Headquarters of Fun. Life there is
very different. Life is super. Life is

happy. Life is full of parties! And, of course, parties make messes.

In fact, springtime means one thing and one thing only to the Super Happy Party Bears, and it isn't cleaning. It means parties of the picnic variety.

As Bubs, the voice of party

wisdom, always says, "No one needs to worry about cleaning up after the party if the party never ends."

And so, every morning, the Super Happy Party Bears wake up and order some breakfast—a slice of ultra-crumbly crumb cake and a filled-to-the-brim bowl of jumpin' jelly beans!

Nothing annoys the critters of the Grumpy Woods more.

Except when the bears have a party.

And they are always having a party.

CHAPTER TWO

Ever since spring-cleaning began,

Only one basket per picnic was

the law. Mayor Quill figured it would

cut down on the amount of litter.

The Super Happy Party Bears were

more than happy to follow the rule.

They just used a bigger basket.

23

The cheerful bear-shaped door to the Party Patch was just big enough for the bears to squeeze through with their enormous picnic basket on wheels. The twelve bears gave a "Heave ho!" and the basket burst out the door and down the flower-lined path.

"Did we remember the watermelon?" asked Jigs over the rumble of the basket.

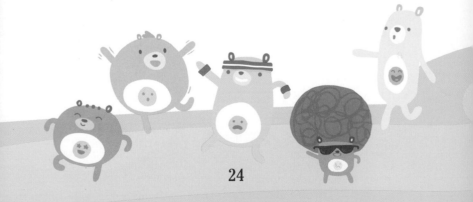

"Yes. What about the hammocks?" asked Mops.

"We have the hammocks," said Shades.

"I hope we have our umbrellas,"

said the littlest bear. "It's going to storm."

"Storm? No way!" said Shades, looking over his star-shaped glasses.

"It *is*," insisted the littlest bear. "A *fun*derstorm!"

Everyone burst into giggles.

"Sunny with a one hundred percent chance of a *fun*derstorm!" cheered Jacks.

The bears paraded alongside the basket as it bumped and rolled across the grass, zigged and zagged between trees, and passed the Grumpy Bramble.

Once they arrived on the banks of the Grumpy River, all the bears got busy setting up the picnic.

From out of the basket
they pulled a heap of colorful
blankets. They laid them out
like a patchwork quilt. On top
of the blankets, they set out all
their favorite picnic foods: fruit
punch, sandwiches, watermelon,

potato chips, pickles, cupcakes, and everything else good for a party picnic. Little Puff carefully displayed her very special "picnic doughnuts," which were iced to look like a checkered picnic blanket. Each one had a candy picnicking townscritter on top.

The townscritters never joined the bears on their picnics, but Little Puff expressed her hope in sugar.

The littlest bear tied a jump rope around his waist and was lowered into the basket by the others to get the last few items: lawn chairs, a barbecue grill, and band equipment—because what's a picnic without music? Before long, the banks of the Grumpy River looked like the Party Patch—if it were shot out of a circus cannon!

Finally, it was time to get the

outdoor celebration under way.
The Super Happy Party Band
grabbed their instruments.

Big Puff hit his drumsticks
together. "ONE, TWO, THREE,
FOUR!"

But before the song started, a large wave erupted from the river, splashing the bears.

"This *fun*derstorm tastes like river water," giggled the littlest bear, catching drops on his tongue.

Jigs held one of her maracas up to her ear to inspect it. "How did we do that?"

"We didn't," said Ziggy. "They did." He pointed his guitar at a group of eight sloths floating on their backs in the Grumpy River.

"NO! NO! NO!" yelled a frog into a megaphone. He was hopping back and forth on the shore. "I SAID *GRACEFUL*! THERE IS NO SPLASH IN *GRACEFUL*! TRY IT AGAIN!"

The bears dropped everything and rushed down to get a closer look.

The frog hit the PLAY button on a boom box. It played a soft and soothing tune as the sloths moved gracefully together through the water. It was like a slow version of the Super Happy Party Dance.

Swim to the right.

 Flop to the left.

Spin, spin, sink.

36

 Pop back up.

The bears burst into applause
when the sloths stopped.

"TAKE FIVE," shouted the frog
to the sloths. He hopped over to
the bears. He was squinty-eyed and
talked from the side of his mouth.
He looked the bears up and down
and, noticing how wet they were,
handed them towels. "APOLOGIES
FOR THE SPLASH. WHEN THEY

GET TIRED, THEY GET SLOPPY,"
he explained, still using the
megaphone, even though the bears
were standing right in front of him.

"I'M COACH RIBBIT AND THESE
ARE THE AQUASLOTHS," he
continued.

Using a megaphone, Coach
Ribbit introduced the sloths. As he

announced each name, the sloth
popped high out of the water and
spun before disappearing once
more beneath the surface.

"DIESEL, CRUZ, ZIP, ACE, DASH,
O'MALLEY, WIZ, AND TAZ."

O'Malley did not pop high out of
the water like the others. Instead,
he removed his swim cap and

bounced and bobbled, doing a "get

all the water out of my ears" dance.

The frog shook his head and

sighed, then turned to the bears.

"MIND TELLING ME WHERE WE ARE?"

"You're in the Grumpy Woods," said Mops.

"INTO THE MEGAPHONE PLEASE!" said the frog, who then turned his megaphone around and held it up to his ear.

Mops leaned in and repeated into the megaphone, as if it were a microphone, "THE GRUMPY WOODS."

Coach Ribbit looked at the map on his clipboard. He turned

the megaphone back to his mouth. "FINALLY. WE'VE BEEN TRAVELING FOR MILES. SOME NICE BEAVERS POINTED US IN THIS DIRECTION. THEY SAID THERE IS A BIG SYNCHRONIZED SWIMMING TOURNAMENT HAPPENING HERE TOMORROW AFTERNOON."

"Ooh, I love swimming!" said the littlest bear.

"IT'S SUPER HAPPY SWIMMING TIME!" the bears chanted, and they did their Super Happy Party Dance as if they were swimming in the water.

Slide to the right...

 Hop to the left.

Shimmy, shimmy, shake.

Strike a pose.

"YOU BEARS ARE GOOD,"
marveled the frog. "OF COURSE,
YOU MUST BE A TEAM."

"Absolutely," said Jacks.

"We're the Super Happy Party
Bears," cheered the bears.

"Teamwork makes the dream
work," said Bubs.

"LOOKS LIKE THOSE BEAVERS

WEREN'T JUST TRYING TO GET RID OF US, AFTER ALL," said the frog over his shoulder to the sloths. To the bears, he said, "WE'RE GOING TO NEED TO REST UP BEFORE WE TRAIN TOMORROW MORNING. ANY IDEA WHEN THE OTHER TEAMS ARE ARRIVING?"

Just then, as if on cue, the townscritters appeared, marching in a straight line. They were feverish with spring-cleaning.

Dawn was leading the pack with her own megaphone in hand, shouting directions. "Sweep to the

right. Dust to the left. Spray, spray, scrub. Repeat."

They moved like a well-oiled machine. Or like a synchronized swim team.

CHAPTER THREE

To the AquaSloths and Coach Ribbit, it looked like a very determined dance team was marching through the Woods.

When the townscritters saw the picnic mess all over the banks of the Grumpy River, they froze.

The AquaSloths and Coach Ribbit
thought the townscritters were
holding for applause. So, they
applauded, and the bears joined in.

"Quilly!" cheered the bears.

"What in the Windex is going
on?" barked Mayor Quill.

"We have new friends!" said the
littlest bear.

"They're a team!" said Little Puff.

"Just like us," added Jacks.

"You didn't hear this from
me," whispered Squirrelly Sam to
Mayor Quill, "but T-E-A-M stands

for 'Together Everyone Achieves Mess.'"

"MESSY! MESSY! MESSY!" sang Dawn Fawn, dropping her megaphone and rocking back and forth.

"Wow," whispered Coach Ribbit, "I didn't even think to add singing to our routine." And then into his megaphone, "IMPRESSIVE MOVES. ALLOW ME TO—"

"Allow you to skedaddle," interrupted Mayor Quill. "My *team* and I have a lot of cleaning up to do."

"WHAT'S THAT YOU SAY?" said the frog.

"MY TEAM IS GOING TO CLEAN UP."

"CLEAN UP AT THE COMPETITION. HA! WE'LL SEE ABOUT THAT!" said the coach.

"You have broken several mayoral decrees," said Humphrey Hedgehog, flipping through the papers on his clipboard so he would look extra official.

"WHAT'S THAT YOU SAY?" said the frog, turning the megaphone around to hear better.

"Unbelievable," harrumphed Humphrey. "YOU BROKE SEVERAL MAYORAL DECREES!"

"YOU WANT TO TAKE TO THE SEAS?" asked Coach Ribbit. "OH, SAY NO MORE. THE RIVER IS ALL YOURS. WE'LL GET OUT OF YOUR WAY."

"You have precissssely thirty sssssecondssss to SSSSCRAM!" added Sherry.

The sloths crawled out of the water as everyone watched. One by one. Slowly. Imagine the speed of

a tortoise and then slow it down.

A lot.

"Thissss issss hardly

sssscramming," said Sherry.

The frog chuckled. "GOOD LUCK

GETTING SLOTHS TO SCRAM.
THEY MIGHT BE GRACEFUL AND
SWIFT IN THE WATER, BUT ON
LAND, FORGET ABOUT IT!"

The quills on the mayor's back
began to quiver, forecasting a quill
storm. He turned the megaphone
around and yelled into it. "NOISE
POLLUTION IS STILL POLLUTION!
STOP YELLING!" He stuffed the
megaphone with garbage before
handing it back to the frog.

"I do apologize," said the frog
in a normal voice. "I've lost my

hearing over the years because of all the yelling. But when working with sloths, yelling is essential."

Just then, O'Malley let out a yawn that seemed to start at the tips of his back three toes and move little by little through his hairy body. Soon the AquaSloths were all yawning. And then they started speaking very slowly.

"Cooaach," said Wiz. "I aam sleeeepy."

"Soo aam I," said Ace.

"Mee, toooo," said Diesel and Cruz.

"Muust snooooze," added Zip,
Dash, and Taz.

O'Malley was already sound
asleep.

"What are they doing?"
Humphrey panicked.

"I told you yelling was essential. This happens whenever I don't use the megaphone," said Coach Ribbit. "Don't mind us. We'll just slumber here. Shouldn't be longer than a few hours."

"Slumber?!" said the bears. "We LOVE slumber parties!"

"The more the merrier. These guys love to snuggle," said the frog. He turned to the townscritters. "Feel free to carry on with your rehearsal."

"FLOPSY MOPSY! FLOPSY

MOPSY! I NEED MY MOP," sang Dawn Fawn, noticing the puddles and clumps of hair left behind as the sloths crawled into a sleeping pile.

"You cannot sleep here," said Bernice Bunny, before she scurried to hide behind the mayor. She disliked being used as Dawn Fawn's mop.

"The tournament's tomorrow," said Coach Ribbit. "After that, we, and our hair, will be out of your hair."

Mayor Quill couldn't take it anymore. He stomped his foot. He shook from head to toe. Just before

the mayor exploded, Humphrey rolled into a defensive ball. The rest of the towncritters ducked behind the enormous picnic basket.

Quills exploded everywhere. Several shot into the Grumpy River. One zoomed straight into Coach Ribbit's megaphone and popped the garbage out in a kind of litter explosion.

"Wow," whispered the frog. "Maybe we shouldn't have cut the confetti cannon from the routine."

Squirrelly Sam pushed his glasses up on his nose and stuck his face into Dawn's megaphone. "YOU'D BETTER LEAVE!" The sloths stirred from their slumber, but they were moving very slowly.

"I have an idea," said Jacks.

He dashed to Party Patch and

returned with eight skateboards.
"The AquaSloths can use these for
quicker crawling."

The sloths lay on their bellies
on the skateboards and pushed
themselves along. It was really
quite genius.

"TO PARTY PATCH!" cheered the
bears.

CHAPTER FOUR

"IT'S SUPER HAPPY SLUMBER

TIME! SUPER HAPPY SLUMBER

TIME!" chanted the bears as

they paraded the AquaSloths on

skateboards through the Woods.

On wheels, the sloths were very

speedy. Coach Ribbit sat on Ace's

back. Taz had drifted off to sleep again, so Big Puff tied the jump rope to the front of his skateboard and pulled the napping sloth along.

"I HAVEN'T MET ANYONE AS INTO SLUMBERING AS YOU BEARS. ARE YOU SURE YOU'RE NOT PART SLOTH?" asked Coach Ribbit into his megaphone. He was yelling because it was important to keep the other sloths awake until they arrived at the Party Patch. The bears had only one jump rope.

"Slumber parties are the best!" said Shades.

"The pillow fights!" said Mops.

"The games!" added Jigs.

"The snacks!" said the littlest bear.

"I liike snaa—" started Diesel. But before he could finish the sentence, he yawned and his eyelids drooped.

"WE LOVE SNACKS!" cheered the bears, causing Diesel to open his eyes and keep crawling.

Once everyone got to the Party

Patch, Coach Ribbit excused himself. "While you are slumbering, I'll go check out some good rehearsal spots. Looks like that other team wants to hog the river." He hopped off.

Ziggy cranked up his amplifier. "ARE YOU READY TO SLUMBER?"

The bears and the sloths cheered.

"I CAN'T HEAR YOU!"

Everyone cheered again.

Big Puff hit his drumsticks together. "ONE, TWO, THREE, FOUR!"

The bears had the best
slumber party they could.

And so did the sloths.

The party was a real snoozer.

CHAPTER FIVE

Every night, all night, Mayor Quill
had one dream and one dream
only. He was sitting at a really
big wooden desk polishing a
very shiny nameplate that said
PRESIDENT QUILL in gold. Humphrey,
dressed like a court jester, brought

him all his fan mail. The rest of the
dream was Mayor Quill reading
the adoring messages from his
citizens. Often there would be
blueprints for a sculpture of Mayor
Quill's face that was being added
to Mount Rushmore.

Mayor Quill loved this dream.
But this morning the dream took

a turn when he stood up from his presidential desk and adjusted his tutu. His tutu? Yes. His tutu.

He began to dance as a voice shouted instructions at him.

SPLIT.

TURN. SPIN.

POOF!

Mayor Quill woke from his

dream-turned-ballet-nightmare and

quickly checked to make sure he wasn't wearing a tutu.

He was relieved to find that he was wearing his official mayoral pajamas. He gave his teddy bear, Senator Fluffy, one last squeeze before getting out of bed.

He stretched. Spring-cleaning sure was hard, and every quill on his body seemed to creak and crack from all the work the day before. What he needed was a dip in his private, members-only watering hole, of which he was the only member. He would ask Arlo

Rabbit, kicker extraordinaire, to
make the whirlpool exceptionally
whirly today to soothe his aches
and pains.

He had just picked up his towel
when he heard it again.

"LEAP. LEAP. ROLL. SPLIT. TURN.
SPIN."

The mayor gasped. It was the
same ballet-yelling voice from his

nightmare. And it was coming from his watering hole.

"LEAP. LEAP. ROLL. SPLIT. TURN. SPIN. AGAIN!"

Mayor Quill tiptoed toward the door, careful not to start dancing like he had done in his dream.

He was about to put his ear to the door to listen when there was a knock on it.

Knock, knocky, knock-knock.

He knew that knock.

The door opened a crack.

"Mayor Quill, sir?" It was Humphrey.

"What do you want?" the mayor barked. "I'm heading to the bath."

"I figured as much, sir," said Humphrey through the crack in the door. "But there seems to be a little problem."

"As stated in Mayoral Decree number seven hundred and two point two, the mayor does not solve problems until after his

Mayoral Decree
702.2

The mayor does not solve problems until after his morning bath.

Mayor Quill

morning bath," said the mayor.

He grabbed his rubber duck,

Congressman Quackers, and

barged past Humphrey.

"What I mean, sir—"

"WAK! WAK!" objected

Congressman Quackers, over the

mayor's shoulder. That's rubber duck language for "go away."

But just as Mayor Quill reached for the doorknob to his bath, the door swung open and out came the littlest bear. He was wearing swim goggles, floaties, and a bathing suit.

"Good morning, Quilly!" the littlest bear said, his tiny paws

splishing and sploshing as he walked away. "Making a doughnut run. Teamwork makes me hungry."

"LEAP. LEAP. ROLL. SPLIT. TURN. SPIN. AGAIN!"

There in the mayor's private, members-only watering hole, a synchronized swimming practice was going strong. Coach Ribbit,

the Super Happy Party Bears, and
the AquaSloths were all there. Arlo
Rabbit was sitting in the corner
reading a magazine. When he saw
the mayor, he shrugged and went
back to reading.

   While the AquaSloths
practiced their routine with deep
concentration, the Super Happy

Party Bears played some sort of game with a beach ball. They were focused, too. But only on fun.

"Pass to Quilly!" said Mops as he bumped the ball higher into the air and straight for the mayor. The ball landed on his prickly head with a *POP!* and a *ffffssssshhhhhhh*.

CHAPTER SIX

Mayor Quill never got his bath.

With the help of Arlo Rabbit's

large and powerful back feet, he

successfully kicked every bear,

sloth, and yelling frog out of his

watering hole.

But soon City Hall was swimming

with complaints about too many sloths. It seemed the mayor wasn't the only one to find himself caught up in the AquaSloths' cross-training, napping, and practicing. They were everywhere!

Mayor Quill called a town meeting.

He stood behind his podium, clutching his towel with one paw and Congressman Quackers with the other. The deflated beach ball still hung loosely from his top quills. Since the mayor had no

extra paw for banging his gavel to

start the meeting, the rubber duck

helped.

"Wak! Wak! Wak!"

"My library branch is ruined!"

cried out Bernice.

"Did you not hear Congressman

Quackers?" asked the mayor. "This meeting is coming to order. You do not have the floor to speak."

But Bernice continued. "I was re-shelving some books when suddenly I was dripped on. My books are water-warped!"

The mayor attempted once again to bring silence to the room. "Wak! Wak! Wak!"

"Really, Bernice," said Humphrey. "There are bigger issues here than wrinkly books. Issues like *privacy*."

"That's not all," Bernice continued. "The sloths were fast asleep, hanging in the tree above, drying themselves off like laundry!"

"Order!" scolded Quill.

"That's enough, Bernice," said Humphrey.

"They did *not* have their *swimsuits* on," explained Bernice.

The group gasped. Dawn Fawn fainted.

Frantic murmurs bubbled up from the gathered bunch.

"No swimsuits?"

"What were they wearing, then?"

"It's indecent."

"Please! Everybody! One at a time," yelled Mayor Quill, repeatedly squeezing Congressman Quackers. "Wak! Wak! Wak!"

"Well, you didn't hear it from me," said Squirrelly Sam, "but Sherry was run over by one of their skateboards."

Sure enough, Sheriff Sherry's back end was bandaged. "I wrote them all sssspeeding ticketssss."

"It looks like they are going really slow," explained Sam, "but then you freeze and you stare and before you know it, they smack right into you."

"And sssseveral of them have fallen asssleep on their wheelssss," said Sherry. "It'ssss ssssuper dangeroussss."

"I'd rather have them sleep on their skateboards than in my bed!" shrieked Opal Owl from the back of the room. "I haven't slept all day long. Not toOOOO mention, they snore!"

"Clearly, we have a problem here," said Mayor Quill. "And we need to solve this problem as we always do in the Grumpy Woods."

"Unwelcome them!" said Humphrey, proudly pulling a giant, dust-covered sign from a nearby closet. It was drippy and spiky and *un*welcoming.

"Haven't we tried this before?" asked Bernice.

Everyone grumbled about it, but no one had a better idea, so they trudged off to find those pesky sloths and get rid of them once and for all.

CHAPTER SEVEN

The townscritters paraded behind
Mayor Quill, who was holding the
*un*welcome sign. They searched
every branch of every tree looking
for napping or air-drying sloths.
They checked Opal Owl's house.
They carefully looked both ways
before crossing any path, for fear

of SWNS (skateboarding while
napping sloths). Just when they
were ready to give up, a voice
echoed through the trees.

"INTRODUCING TEAM
AQUASLOTHS! DIESEL, CRUZ,
ZIP, ACE, DASH, O'MALLEY, WIZ,
AND TAZ."

The sound of distant applause
followed.

"They are at the Grumpy River,"

said Humphrey. "C'mon, let's hurry. Single file."

The townscritters hopped and skittered across the grass, zigged and zagged between the trees, and passed the Grumpy Bramble. When they reached the riverbank, they stooped down to hide in the tall grasses.

"A ssssneak attack issss besssst," said Sherry.

"We will wait for the perfect moment," said Bernice.

"We must move like a unified front," said Humphrey. "All lined up side by side. We will look more intimidating then."

Everyone nodded in agreement.

Coach Ribbit made another

announcement on his megaphone.
"INTRODUCING TEAM SUPER
HAPPY PARTY BEARS!"

Again, applause followed.

The bears lined up along the
river, wearing matching swim
costumes. And they did their Super
Happy Party Dance.

Slide to the right.

Hop to the left.

Shimmy, shimmy,
shake.

SPLASH!

More applause erupted.

"Can we *un*welcome the bears once and for all, too?" asked Humphrey. "These shenanigans have been going on for way too many books now."

"Let's go," said Mayor Quill.

"Remember, unified front."

"I BELIEVE WE DO HAVE ONE MORE TEAM TO INTRODUCE," Coach Ribbit said into the megaphone. "BUT THEY DON'T SEEM TO BE HERE YET."

Just then, the townscritters walked out of the tall grasses, with arms linked and legs moving in perfect rhythm. They looked like they were about to do a kick-line. Mayor Quill stood in the middle, holding the *un*welcome sign high above his head.

"HERE THEY ARE!" announced the frog, making his eyes extra squinty to read the sign. "INTRODUCING TEAM

UNWELCOME!" To himself he
mumbled, "Sounds about right."

The townscritters lined up, as
the Super Happy Party Bears had,
along the riverbank.

"We are here to *un*welcome you,"
said Mayor Quill.

To the surprise of the critters,
everyone applauded.

"Guess these guys are less
popular than we thought,"
whispered Humphrey.

"We are here to clean up," added
Dawn Fawn with a scowl.

More applause.

"ALL RIGHT, ALL RIGHT. LET'S SAVE IT FOR THE CONTEST, SHALL WE?" said Coach Ribbit. "NOW IF THE THREE TEAMS WILL PLEASE TAKE THEIR PLACES, WE CAN BEGIN."

"Wait a minute, what?" asked Mayor Quill. But Coach Ribbit did not hear him. So, Mayor Quill grabbed the megaphone. "WHAT DO YOU MEAN, THE CONTEST?"

"It's time for the swimming tournament," explained Jacks.

"I made costumes for you,"
added Little Puff.

"We are NOT participating in any
tournament," said Mayor Quill.

"But we need three teams to make
it official," said the littlest bear.
"The winner gets to move on to the
next tournament down the river."

"The winner leaves?" asked
Humphrey. "Follow me, Team
Unwelcome. I think I have an idea."

CHAPTER EIGHT

Soon after, the three teams gathered beside the Grumpy River.

"I feel ridiculous," said Mayor Quill, pulling at his swimsuit. "This thing is too tight and my quills are poking through."

Only Sam seemed to enjoy being

in costume. He kept twirling and rolling with excitement. "Gotta stay limber," he said. "I want to win a medal."

"That is not part of the plan," corrected Humphrey. "The sloths must win. Then they will go away. We are simply going to lose the tournament."

"But I've never won anything!" whined Sam. "I want a medal so badly I can taste it!"

"Can I point out the obvious?" said Opal. "I don't swim."

"No worries," said Humphrey.
"You are our aerial acrobat. Just fly overhead and dive down once in a while like you are picking up prey."

Sam and Opal made eye contact. "Now that's a medal I can taste," said Opal. She winked. Sam gulped.

"FIRST UP IS TEAM SUPER HAPPY PARTY BEARS!" announced Coach Ribbit.

Tunes hit PLAY on her boom box, and a surf remix of "If You're Happy and You Know It" filled the air.

The bears

got in the water and formed a circle

around Big Puff, who clapped out,

"ONE, TWO, THREE, FOUR!"

After that, it's difficult to

describe what happened.

Some bears flapped

their arms, wildly

splashing

water

everywhere.

Other bears

posed like water

119

fountains, spraying water into
the air from their mouths. And
some bears bounced up and down
rowdily, causing big, giant waves.
When the song stopped, the bears
exited the water and bowed.

Everyone politely applauded.

"What in the tidal wave was that?" mumbled Mayor Quill.

"THANK YOU, TEAM PARTY BEARS," said Coach Ribbit. "NOT WHAT WE WOULD CALL SYNCHRONIZED, BUT VERY ABSTRACT AND CREATIVE. NEXT UP, TEAM AQUASLOTHS!"

One by one, the AquaSloths slid into the river on their bellies, as the frog hit PLAY on the boom box. Ballet music filled the air, and the swimming sloths created elegant shapes with their long arms,

bodies, and legs. Slowly and gently, they moved like the different colors in a kaleidoscope.

The bears cheered and held up signs reading LIFE IN THE SLOTH LANE and GO AQUASLOTHS! The bears even did the wave.

The AquaSloths swam in a circle

with one leg raised straight up out
of the water. Then they reversed
and swam in the opposite direction
with the other leg high above
them. Then they disappeared into
the water and reappeared on the
surface in the shape of a Party Bear.
The crowd went wild. Coach

Ribbit made eye contact with
Mayor Quill and winked. Mayor
Quill did not like being teased.

"WELL DONE, TEAM
AQUASLOTHS," said Coach Ribbit
into the megaphone. "NOT SURE

HOW TO BEAT THAT. BUT LET'S SEE WHAT TEAM UNWELCOME DOES."

If there is one other thing besides being teased that Mayor Quill does not like, it's being challenged. And with Coach Ribbit's boastful words, something in him snapped.

"Come on, team," he said, adjusting his swimsuit. "Game on."

CHAPTER NINE

Mayor Quill was actually an exceptional swimmer. His quills lay down flat as he cut through the water. He was determined to win. He gave it his all.

But one determined teammate does not a winning team make.

You see, Humphrey was still
planning to lose, and so he spent
the entire routine banging into
other townscritters and getting
water in their eyes. Opal swooped
down several times and picked up
Sam. His screams of "DON'T EAT
ME" echoed off the trees. And the

others, well, they were just plain confused as they splashed about.

After the competition, the three teams anxiously awaited the results.

"WhoOOOO won?" asked Opal.

"You didn't hear this from me," said Sam, "but I don't see any judges." And he was right. In all the excitement, no one had bothered to judge the contest.

"We're all winners!" cheered the bears.

"There has to be ONE winner!" insisted Mayor Quill.

"We should vote," said Humphrey. So they did.

In the end, the AquaSloths won by a landslide with nineteen votes. The Super Happy Party Bears received seven votes, and the

townscritters only two—from

the littlest bear and Mayor Quill.

Taz didn't vote, having fallen

asleep.

"WAY TO GO, TEAM

AQUASLOTHS," said Coach Ribbit.

"OUR NEXT TOURNAMENT AWAITS."

"But first, we must celebrate," cheered the bears.

The Super Happy Party Band played some sleepy tunes perfect for napping and snuggling. The townscritters were so pleased that the sloths were going to leave that they even partied a bit themselves.

The bears took turns being flown high above the river in Opal Owl's talons and then doing belly flops into the water below.

Sherry Snake made a perfect life preserver for the littlest bear to wear into the water. Mayor Quill demonstrated his swim moves for Coach Ribbit, as the frog took notes on his clipboard.

It was a good time for all. But

soon it was time to say good-bye
and send the AquaSloths down the
river to the next tournament.

All the bears got one last sloth
hug.

Coach Ribbit shook Mayor
Quill's paw. "You know, you could

have a future in synchronized
swimming. Look me up if you ever
need a coach."

"IT'S SUPER HAPPY QUILLY
TIME! SUPER HAPPY QUILLY
TIME!" cheered the bears, and
they did their Super

Happy Party Dance. And you know what?

The townscritters danced, too.

They were feeling just a *little less grumpy*. THE END.

ABOUT THE AUTHOR

In previous chapters, Marcie Colleen
has been a teacher, an actress, and
a nanny, but now she spends her
days writing children's books! She
lives in her very own Party Patch,
Headquarters of Fun, with her husband
and their mischievous sock monkey
in San Diego, California. Occasionally,
there are even doughnuts. This is her
first chapter book series.

Don't Miss the other SUPER HAPPY PARTY BEARS Books